Duff Gyr is a retired educator in international education,
with writing as a personal ritual of exploration
and reflection.

To my family and to Monique Levrat, the dream catcher.

Duff Gyr

TRUTH AND DEBRIS

AUSTIN MACAULEY PUBLISHERS™

LONDON • CAMBRIDGE • NEW YORK • SHARJAH

Copyright © Duff Gyr 2023

The right of Duff Gyr to be identified as author of this work has been asserted by the author in accordance with sections 77 and 78 of the Copyright, Designs and Patents Act 1988.

All rights reserved. No part of this publication may be reproduced, stored in a retrieval system, or transmitted in any form or by any means, electronic, mechanical, photocopying, recording, or otherwise, without the prior permission of the publishers.

Any person who commits any unauthorised act in relation to this publication may be liable to criminal prosecution and civil claims for damages.

This is a work of fiction. Names, characters, businesses, places, events, locales, and incidents are either the products of the author's imagination or used in a fictitious manner. Any resemblance to actual persons, living or dead, or actual events is purely coincidental.

A CIP catalogue record for this title is available from the British Library.

ISBN 9781035807925 (Paperback)
ISBN 9781035807932 (Hardback)
ISBN 9781035807956 (ePub e-book)
ISBN 9781035807949 (Audiobook)

www.austinmacauley.com

First Published 2023
Austin Macauley Publishers Ltd®
1 Canada Square
Canary Wharf
London
E14 5AA

Chapter 1

The new generation is sober in orientation: The last 40 years don't exist and before us is a clear and tough future quite unconnected with anything.
It will be—as is already suspected—short.
It won't be long before it starts tossing madly like a tin can on a cat's tail
tied to the shambles of a world divided between the winners who lost and are
running around searching for their missing victory and the ones who in the end will foot the bill.
(Zbynek Fiser alias Egon Bondy)

My father's apparition pulled me with it outside of time. We bury our dead and expect from them no further interference in our lives. We construct our memories out of fragments or we forget completely. But we lose the solid ground on which we expect to walk when the dead come back to life and blow our constructions to rubble.

For 25 years, I had thought that my father was dead. Seeing him again sent me into an accelerating tailspin. It started with a tightening chest, breathing cut with a tourniquet of spiralling time. It ended with a collapse. I had been building in a zone of high seismic activity. For the second time, I was a patient in a psychiatric clinic.

Now I am out, on my own to pick up the pieces and reconstruct, but there is not much building material left. In the distance are the shards of shattered structures. I am looking at those that are close at hand, picking slowly through the recent past. I work backwards, taking solace in what I have done to help others and slowly turning to my own salvation. Stories, shared, may be all that I have as a foundation.

At work, I walk through school halls and the ringing sound of children's laughter projects me into the multiple echoes of my own childhood. The time and space between Czechoslovakia in the 60s and Vancouver at the start of a new century have collapsed. I now find myself staring continuously into the mirror, trying to recognise the person that I am and to catch glimpses of the people that I have been. If I believe my eyes, the face in the mirror is round with only fine grey-blonde hair on the top. My scales say that I am light, and my eyes see thin but I feel heavy. I've seen pictures of refugee women with all that they own, plus perhaps a child or two, piled upon their backs. This is what I see in the mirror in the morning. In the evening, if I have been able to be helpful to someone during the day, I imagine that I can see a crinkled smile.

Petr told me I was beautiful. We were young; he wasn't handsome. He had a face marked with acne, but he had been an outlaw, and that attracted me. I have now seen too much internal darkness to dwell long on surfaces. I have worked to neutralise my physical attraction. Only now do I realise that in neutrality, I can never win. My work involves helping other people, mostly children, look through their baggage. The reigning prince told me that I had the best job in the building. He calls me the Dream Catcher, and everyone refers to me as DC. I accept the name but feel that as often as not, I catch nightmares. The principal in our school is always referred to as the prince. Each prince has seemed a part of a royal family that is out of touch with the people that they serve. New principals try to stay in touch but they slip away as they become administrators. They prance in full of new ideas, stay with us for a while, and then due to exhaustion or the offer of higher pay, they move on, leaving the place little changed. I and a few other stalwarts stay and see generation after generation of our efforts graduate and move on.

My job has been to collect the stories of each individual. If they are students, they may start to tell me their stories at the age of five when they first come for kindergarten; only some stop telling me them when they graduate at 18. My stories come in four-part harmony: students, teachers, the prince, and parents. Everyone else hears only part of this symphony; I am the only one lucky enough to hear the whole. They all talk and I listen; carefully, and sometimes I take notes. I may respond with questions that lead them to some temporary denouement, but usually it seems that just listening does that. They call me the school psychologist.

Most of the stories, I remember. I did take notes on them all and, with a keyword or name, the whole comes back. This collection is my treasure chest, these stories my jewels. Some are hardened by heat and pressure to the density of a diamond. Many of the stories formed their richness through the sedimentation of many years.

Professional secrecy has prevented me from talking much about these stories to others. I have respected the privacy of each story, especially my own. As a child, I heard the Hussite expression, "In spite of everything, the truth prevails." This did not tend to be the case in the Czechoslovakia of my youth. In general, I find that we have to dig for any truth that we hope to find.

Powers of oppression in the world fight against the free spirit and truth. Perhaps most of the oppression is internal. The truth of my stories, and most others, is buried beneath tons of debris.

Now I would like to use the stories of others as tools to uncover the verity of my own, stories as crowbars, jackhammers and cranes to lift away the debris. Finally, stories as gloved hands to gently place remains into a resting place of honour and respect.

Chapter 2
Every Single One of His Stones

It's extremely short-sighted to believe that the face society happens to be presenting to you at a given moment is its only true face. None of us knows the potentialities that slumber in the spirit of the population, or all the ways in which that population can surprise us when there is the right interplay of events, both visible and invisible.
Vaclav Havel

Alex came to me in his first days at school as a 12-year-old that had been placed in a class of ten-year-olds because of his poor reading. He walked quietly into my office and introduced himself with the assurance of an adult. Alex was tall for his age, solid, and moved with agitated grace. He looked at the collection of puzzles that I kept on my desk and solved one in a few seconds without thinking about it. He looked at my collection of books and said, "You read stuff like, Gramps."

"Do you like to read?" I asked.

"I learnt how this summer."

"Tell me how you learnt."

"I just started. Gramps taught me how to fish and then how to read," he replied.

"Gramps must be very special," I said, wondering how reading could be connected to fishing. "He has time. My parents sent me to Gramps because the school asked me to leave. The principal said that they had no more solutions. Mom and dad didn't have the time to keep me, but Gramps lives alone in his old house in the mountains. He doesn't go to work. He has all the work he needs at home."

Alex stood up, walked over to the open window and took a deep breath of air. "Alex, what do you mean when you say that the school had no more solutions? What sort of problems were you causing?"

"I was causing every kind of problem. So much that my mother used to call me a monster. She said it in front of me when we met the old school principal on the first day of school. I was bad; all the students told me so, told me over and over again. I was stupid. The teacher didn't say it, but I felt it when I couldn't read, and every day I felt it again and again." Alex sighed, turned towards me, cracked his knuckles, stretched his neck and slumped down in the chair in front of the desk again.

"No one knew what to do with me. People would not invite me over because I broke their toys, I spilled the food, I made too much noise and I never sat still. Teachers kept telling me that they could not get my attention. I couldn't do what they asked, so I did anything, and it always bothered them. It wasn't really my fault. I didn't mean to do bad things. It just seemed that whatever I did people would get upset, and that made it worse.

"Only Gramps knew what to do with me. He wouldn't say anything about me. He wouldn't try to do anything for me. He would do his own stuff and ask me for help if he needed it.

When I would see him getting out his tools, I would come over but I was careful not to make a mess because one time when I did, he knocked me over with a backwards fist but without a word. I would go up the mountain behind him to fix his fences and I would give him a hand when he asked for it. We didn't talk often. He would ask for a tool or a hand but mostly he said nothing."

"You're sitting quietly now, Alex," I said. "You're sitting quietly and telling me a very good story. Do your parents give you any medicine to help you be calm?"

"Not anymore. They did at my other school but I still caused problems, and I used to throw away the pills. My parents stopped having me take pills when I went to live with Gramps. He wouldn't let me bring them."

"Your parents were doing what they thought was best for you and they must have had a doctor advise them to give you the pills, but it seems like Gramps must have known better because you are sitting still now without pills." I watched his head come up. He gave me a direct glance and leant back in the chair with his hands behind his head.

"But being with you is like being with Gramps. You're not telling me stuff; you are listening to me. In class now, I still move around, but I can sometimes sit still," he said, sitting up and folding his hands in his lap.

"I am a little surprised to hear that Gramps hit you. He sounds too understanding to do that."

"He is tough and he doesn't like to repeat himself. He only sorta hit me, not hard for him, and only when I didn't pay attention to his words. I didn't forget to do things right the next time. It hurt less when he hit me than when someone calls me stupid.

"When they asked me to leave school no one knew what to do with me, so they called Gramps and he said to bring me up to the cabin. He would be happy to have me, but he wouldn't let me bring along any noisy electronic games.

"When my mother pulled up to the cabin, I jumped out and into Gramps' arms, then down to wrestle with Penny, his dog. Mom got out and gave Gramps a hug and I heard her tell Gramps, maybe in sort of a joke, that I was good for nothing. She said that she and Dad had tried everything and she asked Gramps if he could do anything with me. Gramps said that we would do lots of things together. He said that all he would try to do is to help me focus. My mom said, 'Good luck,' like there was no way he could do that."

Alex sat down, leant forward onto his knees, gave them a tight hug and let his head hang between them for a moment.

I was impressed with the attention to detail that Alex gave to his story. In this modern world, we move at a pace that does not encourage concentration and attention, does not encourage calm or peace of mind. We have children that just cannot sit still; there seem to be more and more of them. Parents don't seem to have the time and can crush a child's exuberance with worry and rules. Power is an uneasy balance for parents and governments. Authority can turn into too much control. I was fascinated by Gramps. "Tell me more about your stay with Gramps," I said.

"At first, it was a bit strange being with him alone. Normally, I stay with him but my parents are there. At night, Gramps' cabin of wood and stone creaked and groaned in the wind, not like our new home in town. He built his own home and he used only stuff that he found in the mountains. He cut his own trees and carried his own rocks.

"I woke up early. Gramps had said that we would walk to the top of the mountain and I would get my own pack. I knew the path a little way already, and at the start, I ran ahead with the dog, Penny. *Gramps is slow,* I thought. I tried to get to the top first, but then I couldn't breathe and he walked slowly past me. I drank from my water bottle. The pack was fun but heavy. When I saw Gramps far ahead, I thought, *Run ahead, run ahead, run ahead.*" Alex leant forward, his hands on his knees.

"But Gramps warned me to take one step after another. He said that we wouldn't arrive before lunch. He told me as I came up to him that I should enjoy each step. He never seems to stop and rest. In order to enjoy every step, I decided to count them. Then I hurried so that I could count faster but tripped and fell over and my bloody knee made me lose count. Gramps told me that counting was a distraction and that it takes from the essence of things. I wondered what distraction and essence meant." Alex stood up and circled the room, turned to look at me, but as I said nothing, he sat down again and continued.

"I like counting and I was good at counting in my old school. At least some things, the teacher wouldn't let me count cookie-sale money anymore 'cause she had to check my counts every time, but I was the fastest in the class.

"I was tired of counting steps and thought I would count all the stones as I walked, but Gramps said that counting stones in the mountains was like counting stars in the sky. He said I should learn to look at them, that I should pay attention to their colour, shape and texture, think about them, how they were different and how the same, and that I should wonder where they come from. He wanted me to think about the stones. I didn't know how or what to think about stones. A stone seems too dead to think about. But I did settle down and puzzle about it for long enough to forget I was walking until we arrived at the top."

I told Alex that I liked collecting stones when I was in the mountains, that people teased me because they always came back with lighter packs after eating and drinking everything that they had brought. But with the stones that I collected mine was always heavier when I came home. I said that I like to decorate my house with stones. I find that they are fascinating and seem heavy with age, and some even showed images of things once alive. "How did it feel to be at the top of the mountain?" I asked Alex.

"After the climb, I was tired. We sat quietly and ate some bread and cheese and I finished up my chocolate. I asked Gramps what a distraction was. He said that a distraction takes your attention away from what is important. I asked how I could know if something was important. He told me that only I could say what was important for me. When I said that Mom thought that it was important to do well in school, he replied that my mom was just telling me what was important for her. Since I wasn't doing well, either it was not important to me, or I was being distracted. When I asked him why I got distracted, he said that an active brain is interested in everything.

"He said that it is hard to calm a wild mind. He pointed to a hawk soaring in slow circles above the valley and said that the trick was to be like the hawk. He said that the hawk finds the rising wind that will carry him high enough to be out of sight of his prey but within the range of his own vision. He does this without a flap of his wings, without effort." Alex spread his arms and closed his eyes. "If I pretend I am a hawk, it seems like I can see everything. It seems like I can slow down and wait for the right moment." He lowered his arms, opened his eyes and let out a slow sigh.

"Your grandfather thinks carefully about things," I said, "and you seem to remember them well. He talked about distraction from essentials. Did you ask him about the word 'essentials'?"

"Gramps told me that it was important to learn to avoid the distractions that prevent me from learning important things like reading and writing. He promised me that up in the mountains with him, I would learn to focus because there were no distractions, only essentials."

"Only essentials, Alex? Gramps lives with only the essentials? Can you think of non-essential things that you live with when you are away from Gramps and the mountains?"

"Well, mostly TV and the things that they make us want to buy. Gramps does not have many things, but he has food, heat in his house and you can take a hot shower. He has everything he needs."

"But what do you do when you are with Gramps and not working? What do you do at night or to play?" I asked Alex.

"There wasn't much to do at Gramps' cabin in the evening—no TV, no electronic games, and no one to play with except Gramps, who didn't play much. He would mostly read in the evening. The walls of the cabin seemed to be made of books. Every room had shelves from ceiling to floor. Gramps seemed to be always talking with whatever book he was reading. When he reads, it's like he is arguing. He underlines and writes. He reads the stuff over again. He is fun to watch.

"Most people had difficulty getting Gramps to talk, but he talks to books. Maybe it's weird. He doesn't have as many children's books as you have."

Alex fanned the pages of one of my books on philosophy.

"My teacher tried to teach me to read but my brain did not seem to move in lines. I would bounce down a page and didn't usually get through any single word, so by the time I would get to the bottom, the letters and words would make knots that my brain was unable to undo. Gramps told me that he would teach me to read. In the beginning, all I did was watch and listen to him. He would talk to me about what he read and read a few lines to see what I would think. Usually, I wouldn't know what to think; the words were so thick. I felt like a bug stuck in honey. Other times, he would read simple stories and I would listen to every word and see everything in my head."

"So he would read and you would listen sometimes. His books were probably difficult. Did he have any books with pictures and just a few words?"

"He did have some with pictures and I started to read them later. He told me that writing was like a picture. He said that I just had to use the words to put the picture together in my head. He told me that in some languages, people built their words out of pictures."

On my desk were some fossils. Alex picked each one up slowly and examined the images fixed like permanent photos in the rock.

"Once when we were outside, we found a fossil of something that Gramps called a Nautilus. He said the stone was once on the bottom of the sea.

"But it's now at the top of a mountain—weird. I am not sure how that happened. He said that the fossils were like the world's first writing. He told me that humans were just learning to read fossils, that they couldn't understand them for thousands of years. He was sure that I would learn to read words in just a few years. Gramps told me that if I relaxed, I wouldn't have knots. He said that reading was like weaving. He said that I had to find the pattern that connected the words."

"The pattern that connects words... Do you know what he meant by that?" I replied.

"Not exactly. One night, I put myself to sleep, wondering about the pattern that connects words. But I got distracted, then fell asleep. From my bed in the morning, I would look at the shapes that the boards make on the cabin's wooden floor. In the air above was sunlight with dust particles that dance, like tiny fish, in an aquarium of light. Early in the morning, Gramps opens doors and windows in the cabin to freshen the stale night air inside. This air makes the dust swirl in every direction. Just before I got out of bed, Gramps would close the windows and doors and I would watch as the dust would settle and still. I hoped that my mind would be still and settle like the dust in this early morning sunlight. I thought maybe with a still mind, I could learn to weave words."

He picked up an Inuit soapstone carving of a whale that curled like a ying-yang symbol into an eagle's head.

"The natives carved those two together because they are the masters of the sea and the air," I said. "As Gramps said, it is not easy to calm a wild mind, but as I have noticed you seem calm now, Alex. Where does that come from?" Alex rubbed the smooth stone and closed his eyes.

"It has to do with what I see and what I say in my head," he said. "I used to say that I was stupid, and then I would tell myself I was smart because I could count better than anyone and draw well, too. I used to fight with myself in my head and have unhappy pictures. Once I said to Gramps at breakfast that if fossils only touched some stones, and that for thousands of years, people did not know how to read them, maybe I was a stupid stone without a fossil. My brain would never read words."

Alex picked up one of my fossils and felt its image. He picked up another that had no fossil but very interesting lines and veins.

"Gramps told me that the words of the Lord were written on every single one of his stones. He said that each stone wasn't a fossil but that some message was in each stone. 'Wise people,' he said, 'had only begun to read the stones.' Gramps said that the message contained in these words was so complex that people could only get a piece of it and it has taken many years to put these pieces into a pattern that we understand. He told me that human words come from human minds and didn't have the same time behind them. I didn't really understand, but when he told me that I wasn't stupid and that learning anything important took a lot of time, I felt better. He said I would read human words when I decided it was important."

I covered his hand as he held the stone. I put both of my hands together on his and looked into Alex's quiet, grey eyes.

"I can see why you might not understand, Alex. Gramps explains things in complicated ways. I suppose it is because he is not used to being with children. He does most of his talking with his books, but if you don't understand, you do seem to remember what he says."

"I remember because he talks slowly and I get the feeling that what he says means something. I think Gramps says important stuff and I want to understand. In the quiet of the cabin, sometimes I would repeat some of his words, like a song, sometimes just before sleep, and that is how I can remember them and tell them to you now."

"How did Gramps teach you how to read?" I asked, curious that what must have been a lack of technique had succeeded where teachers had failed.

"It started with bees," Alex said.

"Your reading started with bees that buzz or the 'B's in the alphabet? What do you mean, Alex?"

"It started with real bees. Breakfast with Gramps was always outside. We would carry a couple of trays filled with butter, jam, homemade bread, a pitcher of juice and a thermos of coffee outside on the table in the sun. As it got colder, we would set the trays on the railing and then wipe the water off the table and chairs. On a morning of beautiful sunlight, I watched as Gramps took out a tiny jar with a bit of jam in it and, with the top off, left it on the edge of the table. The sun was low but starting to get warm. As we ate, a bee got his feet sticky with the jam in the little jar and then flew away. I felt warm as I finished my bread and jam. As I drank my juice, I nearly choked on another bee that was in my glass. Then I noticed that the little jam jar was filled with bees. I asked Gramps where all the bees came from and he said that the first one was attracted by the sweetness and then went off to tell his friends. I asked how a bee could tell his friends and he said that the bee that finds something sweet can tell his friends with a dance. The other bees read where the food is by the speed and the direction that the bee dances. I didn't know how to read, so I asked how a bee could learn and he said that bees don't learn; they just know. That made me feel worse. I wished I could just know how to read. Why did I have to work so hard? He made me feel better by saying that only animals with little brains don't have to learn, but that they only know how to do a few things and they can't change. At the end of breakfast, he put the top tightly on the little jar, covering the bees, put it in his pocket and said he would take me to the river to learn how to fish."

I got puzzled how this could have led to reading but explained, "They call the bee dances circle and waggle dances, Alex. They tell other bees where to find what they need to make honey with a dance. But why did your grandfather put them in a jar?"

"He tricked the bees so he could use them for fishing. With no work, he had bait to catch our food. Not many people use bees for bait, but it works if you do it right, and it was an easy way to get our bait. We carried our fishing poles and we walked along the stream under the trees.

"We stopped where the stream made a pool. Gramps took out the little jar of bees and they were all dead. Gramps showed me how to put one on a hook. The first bee scared me and I broke him into bits. The second time, I got my hook through the big parts and he stayed on the hook. Gramps showed me how to cast the bee into the water. It was difficult; the first two I hooked on the tree behind me, but I was careful the third time and the bee landed on the other side of the stream in a slow spot just under a tree. I was just about to sit down when the pole bent and pulled. I almost let go but Gramps told me to hold on. I saw the fish jump. I think that I jumped as much as the fish as I tried to bring him to shore.

That one got away, but by the end of the day, I had two, and Gramps had three. I never ate much of the fish that Mom makes but those fish were the best I'll ever eat. Gramps said that if I could catch fish, I was ready to learn how to read."

I scratched my head, still puzzled, and asked, "Catching fish and reading are not really the same. What did he mean?"

Alex straightened up. "Both take patience," he said. "Both take patience, and the flow is always in one direction. At home, after we had eaten our fish, Gramps got out a book that was lots of words, all of them a mess of many letters without a single picture in the book. He said that reading a book like that was like fishing a mountain river, with words rushing at you so fast that you cannot stand in front of them. You cannot catch a word if they are rushing by too quickly to see. He took out one of his picture books with only a few words on a page. He said that in a book like that, I could catch each word as it came. I liked the pictures in the book. Gramps had me tell him what they were about. Then he showed me the words on the bottom of the page that I had used myself. With his hand on my shoulder, and his help when I couldn't read a word, I forgot that I didn't know how to read. At the end of the book, he had me write down the words that I recognised. The next day, I opened the book and could still read some of the words. Gramps read with me all morning and we finished the book. That day, Gramps treated me like it was my birthday. We made a cake together and he covered it with candles, each one for a word that I knew. Every morning for the rest of the summer, we spent time looking at books, guessing at words, recognising some, reading and writing them down. We would talk a lot about what the stories were about and go over and over them till I had most of them memorised. By the end of the summer, Gramps had to stop my reading so that he could get some work done and we made many trips down to the library in the valley to find more books for me.

"Mom cried when she heard me read for the first time. I read in the car all the way home and Dad said that he had never thought I could sit still for such a long time. Now I am here. I was scared to come, but when I met the principal, Mom did not call me a monster and the principal listened to me."

Alex's mother came to take him home and interrupted the story that day. Neither he nor I had felt the time go by. The door closed and I dropped into my chair. Why do we make all kids, all people, fit into one mould?

Over time, Alex continued to have a lot to say, often at an inappropriate time, and his teachers would come to me for help. Alex was intelligent, creative, motivated and full of exuberance and energy, but his style of learning does not fit easily into our current model of schools. He was like Czechoslovakia in my youth: full of hope and exuberance but constrained within an inappropriate structure. How should the bursting energy of youth be contained?

When I was a kid in Czechoslovakia, the Soviets decided to control exuberance with an army of 800,000 soldiers. They invaded in the middle of the night. Tanks rolled through the streets. The country was just getting free. It had been a spring time of ideas. But fear took the place of freedom, and free spirits were tortured into denial or death. Generations disappeared under authority.

Alex suffered no such fate. He surprised many of his primary school teachers with his good grades in high school and his help to teachers in the organisation of tutoring support for all students in difficulty. It took time and the contribution of a few dedicated individuals that believed in a potential that few others could see.

Chapter 3
Talent and Frustration

My own earliest memories as a very small child in Prague are of the excitement of big crowds in a soccer stadium. When the fans would rise at the scoring of a goal, I would be surrounded by bodies and couldn't see. My mother would raise me to her shoulders so that I could look out over everyone's head. My father scored most of the goals. The team would carry him from the stadium on their shoulders after a win. They called him the golden head; he stood well above the other players and would often score with a nod of his high forehead.

We spent a lot of time at the soccer stadium and the team would come to our home in the evening. I was the only child. Men would pass me back and forth, hold me on their laps and tickle and tease me. Early in the evening, they would eat and talk. At some point, my father would start to sing and soon everyone would join in. Eventually, everyone would drink, sing and dance. I was special—everyone's little girl. They would pick me up, twirl me around and dance with me. Then it would be bedtime, and my father would tell me a new story made up fresh every night and my mother would sing me a soft song to put me to sleep.

In my dreams, I would return often to the same landscape. I would walk with my parents up a hillside of golden grass and lie at the top under an apple tree, the autumn sun warm before the evening's chill. We would pick the sweet apples and eat them from the tree.

In the dream, it is the end of the season and the apples on the ground add a hint of the smell of decay to the air. As we walk down the hill, my mother is no longer in the dream. I am with my father, walking through open woods and fields. From a distance through high grass, we see two crows pulling at an object on the ground. As we approach, we see that it is a dead deer and the crows are pulling at its anus and intestines. They pull until the digestive tube breaks internally and comes out. They continue pulling at this long inverted tube, eating the clumps of shit as they came upon them. We are disgusted and chase them away. A cloud of flies arises and then resettles. The eyes are gone and the empty sockets are a buzzing mass of flies. I look on, sick with disgust.

The dream changes and I am in our rusted old truck, driving a dusty country road with my father at night. Out of the darkness, we see startled eyes the size of moons and then there is the horrible impact of the deer on the bumper. My father stops, goes out to the ditch beyond the light, picks up a massive stone and I hear the dull thud as he puts the deer out of its misery.

As an adult, I still enjoy listening to stories. At school, I listen to the stories of children and then I stay with them and watch them grow. The stories that I like best are the ones that do not turn out as expected. The expectations come from teachers that are often too quick to make judgments. Some like to think that success or failure in their class will determine the future of a child. I have enjoyed watching many school failures turn into very successful adults, and I have been unhappy enough to see many successful school children suffer through setbacks as they got older.

Samuel was our school's soccer star. At the age of eight, he could keep the ball in the air indefinitely with his feet, knees and head. At 16, his tall, blonde head served as the offensive flag. There is a video that I have kept of Samuel stopping a shot in front of his own goal with a soft, lobbing header picked up by his feet as he accelerated. He passed the ball between the legs of a defender, dribbled around two others as he ran the length of the field and then kicked into the top right corner of the goal with his left foot.

His soccer coach told me once, "I've never seen such a good soccer player at his age."

He also said that if he was not paying attention, Samuel would kick the ball in another kid's face. He was so aggressive, competitive and driven that he could play any position better than any other child the school had ever had. In class, he was just as successful and his talent was just as intimidating to other children. A mother came to complain to me that Samuel would tease her daughter when she read slowly in class. Teachers would complain that he talked back and questioned everything they said. Finally, the prince and I had to intervene when a father came in shouting, "If that kid touches my son again, I'll come to school and take care of him myself."

We calmed the distraught father before he did any damage. We took the two kids into the office and the prince said, "Samuel, you have to set the example. There is no fighting or teasing allowed in this school. Focus your energy on soccer. I can't have parents coming into school to complain about you. You know what the rules are around here and you have to obey them like everyone else. What would happen if everyone behaved like you?"

"We would have a better soccer team and a smarter school," I heard Samuel mutter as he turned away. The prince heard him too and kept him in for detention the next day.

We all looked forward to a golden future for Samuel. I now see him more often than ever. He comes to me for consultation. He comes well dressed and in a beautiful car but he has been divorced twice and he is only just starting to spend time with his adolescent children.

Samuel always reminded me of my father. I saw my father grow frustrated with the inabilities of others. His aggression grew as he repeatedly found his way blocked by uninspired people in a structure that punished initiative. In the end, it seemed that his anger would only subside as he drank it into submission. My early childhood was perhaps idyllic, but memory of a period is shaded, textured and changed by events that follow. When I look back at those early years, I feel like I am looking through darkened lenses.

As a young adult, my father was one of the biggest sports heroes in Czechoslovakia. His rabid temper helped win many soccer games. As a soccer player, my father had been warned a few times that he was being too critical of the Communist party. The warnings became more frequent and serious when he retired from soccer and started working as a reporter for the paper. He didn't keep his job with the local paper for very long but I never heard him make an unhappy remark about that loss. He went to work for a small literary paper that would slip its political comment into book, film and theatre reviews, a practice of *'samizdat'* which allowed news to pass undercover.

The first time that I realised that my father was not well liked by everyone was during his preparation for a speech to the Writer's Union. I was still too young to understand the level of risk he was taking but I was impressed by the emotion he put into the words as he practiced his speech at home. He repeated the conclusion often enough for me to remember it to this day. "Unless the Union takes a critical look at itself and stops its intolerance and inflexibility towards the best writers in the country, Czech writing will be forever condemned to mediocrity." He came home saying that he was given a tremendous applause. He was even more pleased when he heard that the president of the Union had called him a threat.

I can remember him saying, "In a factory of uniformity, anything outside the mould is a threat. Spend your life breaking the industrial mould and freeing the natural animal within."

Schools have been built on the industrial model. Too often, I have seen well-meaning members of school staff trying to force a child into a form that didn't fit. It is like the Chinese tradition of binding women's feet to make sure that they remain small—the result is a disfigurement, a monstrosity.

Chapter 4
Adolescence

On the morning of August 21, 1968, we were awoken by the thunderous sound of Soviet tanks invading our city. We listened in disbelief as we were told by a Radio Prague announcer that the city and country and been invaded by Soviet troops and that the tanks were moving into position to take over the radio station. At one point, the microphone was held outside and we could hear machinegun fire and explosions. Father left to help at the station and we were told to stay inside until he came back. At 11 o'clock in the morning, the radio went off the air and we were left without news of the invasion or from Father. He burst in the door in the evening but stayed only long enough to gulp down some food and to say that he would be helping with the continuous movement of broadcast locations and coordinating resistance through radio announcements. He repeated that we should stay inside and to listen for instructions on the radio.

There had been no military preparation for this invasion. The Czech army stood by as the Soviet invaders physically took over the country. But the Czech people refused to submit. Radio broadcasts would tell us not to confront the soldiers but to resist passively in every way possible. We were told to take off road signs to confuse the invaders. People would co-ordinate the ringing of church bells and the honking of horns at a given time to upset the youthful invaders. The young Soviet soldiers had been expecting to be greeted as a liberating force but instead found themselves confronting the entire civilian population. In every way possible, we did our best to confuse and make uncomfortable our aggressors. Father was never home. We would hear him on the radio and we knew that the broadcast itself proved that he was busy helping to keep the station out of Soviet hands.

My parents had explained to me that the changes in Czechoslovakia were a reaction to twenty years of Soviet repression. In 1948, a communist coup made Czechoslovakia a Soviet satellite and Klemet Gottwald the Czech President. All major businesses were nationalised and farmers were forced to collectivise. From 1948 to 1953, Czechoslovakia went through Stalin-like purges with the development of forced labour camps for dissidents. Antonin Novotny, a former spy for the Gestapo, was made the first secretary of the Communist party in 1953, and then was elected president in 1957. For the first time, the two most powerful positions in the country were in the hands of one man. With little say politically, little possibility for economic gain, and with most production going to feed the Soviet giant, Czechoslovakia entered a period of cultural decline and serious economic problems.

In the late 60s, after more than a decade of repression, Czech artists and writers began to express the growing general discontent with the communist regime. The development of a counter culture of music, art, film and literature reflected a general desire for more openness and accountability from the government. Supported by a universal desire for more freedom, pressure from these dissidents was able to force Novotny out of office and to replace him with two men: Alexander Dubcek, a little known Slovak, who became the new secretary of the Communist party, and Ludvik Svoboda, who became the Czech president. After 20 years of repressive communism, these two leaders accepted public pressure for the development of a 'socialism with a human face'. They were to become the reluctant parents of growth that they could no longer control. Czech society became an unruly adolescent clamouring for power over its own destiny. Behind these two new parents was the shadow of a Soviet bear raising its head from hibernation.

Czechoslovakia and I shared a simultaneous adolescence. During the spring, my height had gone from my mother's nose to her eyes and finally to her equal. The day before the Soviet invasion, I came home from school taller than her. We took a walk together along the swollen banks of the Vltava River to celebrate. The willows along the bank brushed their green branches on the surface of the river, leaving ephemeral lines on the swirling mass of the swell.

My mother held my hand. My fingers were longer and slenderer. Her palms were soft. The back of her hands had scales and wrinkles. Like a young snake, I was growing into my new skin. For the first time, I noticed my mother developing the hint of growing out of her youth.

"What a beautiful woman you have become!" my mother said. "You will have your father's tall, thin body and golden head."

"I hope to have your soft touch and your understanding of people, Mother," I said. Looking at her from above for the first time, I noticed the greying of her hair and the tightening lines around her eyes. Looking into my mother's eyes, I felt as though an umbilical cord of compassion connected us. No longer a connection of nutrients, it was a bridge of support and a filter for pain. Her eyes had the same calming and hypnotic effect as the eddies and pools of the Vlatva River.

I have done my best to forget so much of my adolescence and young adulthood. The images—good and bad—are difficult to bring back. But the feelings, even after 30 years, are still sharp. The memory of my mother's face is no longer clear. I see her completely only in dreams. But I feel her gentle hands and soothing eyes. I try to forget the brutal sound, oily smell and aggressive sight of tanks. I feel the bursting hope of spring and crushing loss at summer's end. I feel my father's strength and sense his weakness. When I close my eyes, I often see him staring at me through prison bars. He reaches out to me but I turn my back and walk away.

Chapter 5
River of Love

As a psychologist, I have spent my life studying cases of abuse, abandonment, repression and frustration.

Linda came to our school at the age of six. We called her 'The Hugger' because she would wrap herself around your legs and cuddle. A United Nations official had rescued her from the horror of a Romanian orphanage. In an environment where many children were tied to their beds to control their wild behaviour, Linda had survived and prospered with a sunny disposition and a therapeutic smile.

When Linda first came to school, at six years old, she couldn't speak a word of English. I was asked to meet her. She came in holding her adoptive mother's hand. She went over to my bookcase, took a picture book and crawled into my lap with it. She looked at me expectantly and touched her fingers to my lips as if she had a magic wand, making a spell for speech. I read in English. She spoke occasionally to explain things to me in Romanian. When her mother came in an hour later, I said that Linda and I had told each other a story.

Linda seemed to possess a genetic disposition for love, refined through environmental necessity. Once, after knowing her for a long time I asked how she managed to remain so cheerful after the suffering that she had been witness to. She replied simply, "My parents are dead, but when I smile, I feel that they are with me." Her optimism was so infectious that we often called her when we had an upset child, particularly if it was a new child that did not understand English.

One dark winter's day, Linda came into my office after lunch and said she had a game that she wanted to play with me. We each took the other by the wrist in a way so as to feel the other's pulse. "I learnt how to slow my own pulse down, and if we do this right, we can slow each other's pulse down. Close your eyes and we will form a circle, a circle of calm. If you think the right things and feel the right way, you can almost forget you are alive," she said.

Through our touch, eyes closed, my mother's eyes came to mind and I felt myself slip into a state of suspended thought. Our silence and contact brought to mind my adolescent walk with my mother.

The grey world that had surrounded us was bathed in green. A setting sun filtered through the forest and its light danced on the ripples of the river. I held my mother's hand and looked down into her eyes and into the spinning circles of the river until I did not know one from the other.

The resounding ring of the cathedral clock bells brought us both back to the needs of the day. "We will be late for making Papa's dinner. He will be angry at our wasting the day."

"This day was no waste," my mother replied, but I felt her hand tighten on mine and her stride lengthen.

With the demand for more openness in Czechoslovakia in the 60s, my father's recognition as a writer was rising. His criticisms of the communists were in the paper, and his voice was on the air. Not often physically present at home but dominating the atmosphere, he was an imposing phantom figure. When we arrived home, my father was at the table eating bread and drinking a beer with one empty bottle in front of him.

"You are already eating," Mother said. "Let me put something better together."

Father stood up, like the unfolding of a clenched fist. "I have little time. I am the speaker tonight."

"Let me quickly—"

"It is too late to do something quickly!" he said as he gathered his affairs.

"As the speaker you need—"

My mother put her hand on his chest but father turned towards the door.

"I needed dinner on time," he said with his hands on the door handle. "We were walking."

"You were talking and forgot! What if I had forgotten I was the speaker? What if the country forgot the reign of terror under Gottwald and the crimes of Novotny? Poor memory is our plague." His anger carried him away and made his speech successful.

By the next morning, we were surrounded by Soviet troops. The world changed forever. We fell into a troubled sleep full of incoherent dreams and nightmares. Czechoslovakia woke from the Soviet slumber in 1989, struggling to piece together memories of the good and bad before the fall. I woke up earlier and escaped into the night.

The Czech leaders were taken to Moscow during the first days of the invasion. They were given a deal that they could not refuse. After three days, all but one of them signed a capitulation and came home in shame. The Czech people, however, had only just begun to resist this infamy. For eight more months, in every possible way, life was made a misery for the invaders. The Soviets captured the country but took a while to gain control of the people. I do not remember any parties from this period or many friends staying for a visit. There was no dancing or singing in the evening. My father would come home late, sit in the kitchen smoking cigarettes and drinking beer. We would find the bottles in the morning but he would be gone.

"Your pulse started at a slow walk and finished in a race," said Linda as we slipped out of our collective trance. "What monster was chasing you?"

Chapter 6
Black Skies

January 16th, 1969 was a dark day. With coal being the major source of heat in Prague, the January skies were a toxic grey. I was at a poorly lit desk, trying to digest the Communist party's censored version of Czech history. Mother was in the kitchen, peeling potatoes.

Father came home early, entering the house bowed like a Sherpa under the tumpline of a tremendous load. He slumped into a kitchen chair, buried his face in his arms and sobbed. We put our hands on his powerful back as he pounded the heavy wooden table with his fists and screamed obscenities at Czech and Soviet politicians, dead and alive.

A student named Jan Palach had burnt himself alive in protest of the Soviet invasion. On January 16th, the 20-year-old student had walked to Wenceslas Square, doused himself with gasoline and, in the name of truth and freedom, had set himself on fire. With burns over his entire body, stoically claiming that his action was a protest not a suicide, he took three days to die. At the moment of his death, the clock was stopped in the hall of the faculty of philosophy of Charles University where Jan Palach had studied. He was the first of many human torches that lit the dark period in Czech history between the Soviet invasion in 1968 and the Velvet Revolution in 1989.

Genius is nothing more than an internal flame. In fear of being consumed, most of us cut off the oxygen to our own fires; genius fans the flames. In schools, most students arrive with a burning desire to learn. Sometimes, we put out the fire in a desire to save the building. Never have I seen a child consumed by the heat of learning like Adam. He ate encyclopaedias, digested the elements and created connections that most of us took several days to understand. If he missed one question on a quiz, he would be in tears, even as an adult. In his excitement to demonstrate his understanding, I have seen him wet his pants. In a class, he would finish a one-hour exercise in 10 minutes and then bounce around the room like a pinball, hoping his brilliance would win him points with others. More often than not, he would only anger his teachers, most of whom had no idea how to deal with a child so unable to sit still.

Watching Adam grow, I couldn't say that his genius was a gift. He was ridiculed for sloppy dress, for his tears and for his wet pants. The mediocre have no idea how to deal with passion.

Frequently, great efforts are made to kill it. Adam was aware that he was out of step with others. His saving grace was his ability to make fun of himself in front of everyone.

At the end of elementary school, students were encouraged to take part in a talent show. We would have endless piano recitals, ballet demonstrations and magic shows. With his exceptional ability at everything, Adam was put last on the bill, as everyone was expecting something special. He marched on to the stage with a drum attached to his waist, playing his own drum roll. He proudly marched to centre stage and stopped next to a chair. He took off his marching drum, invited the prince up on stage, presented him with a stopwatch and said loudly and clearly, "You will now see me do something that you have never seen before… I am going to sit absolutely still and silent for two minutes as timed by the prince. Please start your watch." And he did. At the end of the two minutes, the whole school stood up and gave him a standing ovation and carried him around the room.

My father carried a black flag at the funeral of Jan Palach. We walked silently from Wenceslas Square to Charles University. The square in front of the building and all of the surrounding streets were filled with forlorn faces.

Like many others, my father lost most of his energy to fight after the funeral. Many Czechs were able to develop a protective skin of humour and a sense of the absurd. Father could not listen to the jokes. He no longer laughed and, after a lifetime of amusing others with a tremendous memory for songs, he stopped singing.

Father stopped singing and Mother lost her glow. Her gaze turned inward. Like a collapsing star, she was being crushed by her own gravity to the point that light could no longer escape the weight of her core.

The Czechs are passionate about sport. Perhaps it is the only level-playing field that they have had. My father had been a star and still followed Czech sport very closely. After the Soviet invasion, any international competition which involved the Czechs against the Soviets became a national obsession. With the biggest Czech sport being ice hockey, no event was as closely followed as the competition between the Czechs and Soviets after eight months of Soviet occupation.

On April 17th, 1969, Czech tempers were very high. They won a hockey match against the Soviets. This was a trigger for pent up frustration. The Czechs rioted in the streets after the hockey match.

The Soviets changed tactics. Having seen that physical control over the country was not working. They started to play with psychological control. Individuals suspected of dissident activities were pulled before panels of interrogation. Through emotional blackmail, the weaker individuals were starting to give in. Some of the most well-educated citizens were finding themselves out of work or only given the opportunity to do menial jobs. The ones who gave in, who gave the names of others, were rewarded and put in line for advancement.

Father had to work, but he was blacklisted from any writing. He was hired as a labourer for a construction company, dirty work tearing down old buildings to recuperate the wood for new buildings. He came home every night covered in dust and too tired to write.

In the spring of 1969, my mother started coughing up blood. The winter coal smoke and dampness had infected her lungs. When we took her to the hospital, the doctor spent several hours with her.

He came out and spent a long time talking to my father on his own. At home, Mother was installed comfortably in bed, and Father told me that I would need to do all of the cooking and cleaning. Mother needed lots of rest.

Chapter 7
Happy Hearts Club Banned

When I was 18 my mother died. So did I, or at least a large part of me. My father did not say much about his feelings to me. In the only conversation that I remember on the subject, we were walking along the banks of the Vlatva River in spring, mostly in silence. As we stood at one point under a willow looking at the dark, oily surface of the swollen river, my father said, "We all meet again in the end." He was sweating and smoking a cigarette and looked as grey as his growing ash. I wanted him to hold me then.

After the death of Jan Palach, I had decided that I would become a psychologist. After the departure of my mother, it hardly seemed worthwhile to study at all. Most of the intelligent people in the country were doing menial work or were in prison. It was called 'normalisation'. Evidence of anti-Communist leanings would be presented to the offender, and they would be given the choice of signing a written retraction of all that they had once believed to be true or they could go to prison for 're-education'.

When laws become outrageous, only the outlaws can be trusted. I have seen the problem outlined well even in the scale of our school. A young, tall and handsome prince took over for several years. He was full of strong ideas. He assured me that within a short time, we would have one of the best schools in the country. He was ruthless with anyone that would not share his vision. Life was made a misery for anyone that did not stick to the prince's ideal. Test scores on the state tests did improve and became among the best in the state. But teachers began to consult me with stress problems, and the artwork of most students showed little diversity or creativity.

Out on the back parking lot of the school, the group of cigarette smokers and drug dealers grew tighter. They had to be chased back into school for classes and would drag their feet, laughing and making jokes about the prince, talking as loudly as possible on their way back in. We developed a detention hall and did our best to discourage the most difficult cases from continuing school. Dropout rates went up as fast as test scores. The school test statistics looked good, and the prince was lauded as a miracle maker; he began to spend his time traveling, sharing his vision with others. Within a few years, he was appointed to the Provincial Board of Education and then to the Federal Office for educational improvement.

Soon after my mother died I became close to a Czech dissident. Petr was sort of a student—enrolled in the university but rarely in classes. He spent his time supporting himself with a variety of odd jobs and in continual discussion with small groups of men in a circuit of beer and wine halls. He became an important contact between the worker's union and the students. Not long after I got to know him, he was caught distributing recordings of the dissident music group, *Egon Bondy's Happy Hearts Club Banned*, and was put in prison. The band was the equivalent in Czechoslovakia of Ken Kesey and the Merry Pranksters in America—an alternative culture that did not rebel against the regime but did what it could to happily ignore it. They promoted abnormalisation and were to be frequently beaten and imprisoned for their beliefs. Their struggle would eventually draw the support of Vaclav Havel, would inspire the writing of the Charter 77 and would slowly encourage the downfall of Communist Czechoslovakia.

Petr spent two weeks behind bars, being beaten at any time of day or night. He decided that it was time to move to a country where the hand raised against rock music was a bit lighter.

"Let's leave Czechoslovakia together," were the first words I remember hearing from him when he was released.

"How can we leave? They will be watching every move that you make now."

"I will find a way. Will you come with me?" he asked with a cold hand on mine.

"It is easier for you; you are alone, Petr. If I leave, they will certainly put my father in prison. They are looking for the first excuse." I held his hands together and blew softly on them to warm them up.

Petr straightened up, put his hands on my shoulders and said, "Your father is famous and can look after himself. What threat does he pose them now that he has lost his voice? He cannot publish anything. He does nothing out of line. I will find a way to leave and then we will talk again, maybe even talk to him. He would want you to leave, I am sure. I think that we can make it to Canada."

Chapter 8
The Strength of a Man

As a psychology student in Prague, I would often come home late. One evening, after my father lost his writing job, and my mother had died. I came home to a house with no lights. The door was unlocked and I entered to see only the sharp, small glow of a cigarette in the darkness of the living room. I sat down next to my father.

"They have put me in with the swine," he said.

"Father, not even swine could take the shine from a star," I said, rubbing his back.

"They actually put me in the pig pen with a pile of old wood. They asked me to pull nails from the old planks. The whole day was spent removing hundreds of rusty, useless nails to make sure that they wouldn't dull the planner that would straighten the old planks. I had my feet in pig slop and the sow was in heat and would come to me oinking and squealing for affection, her snout full of slop and grime, an animal twice or three times my weight. In the end, she pushed me over and I was covered in the shit. My foreman came over, a 20-year-old kid. He is a local hero because he has won medals for weight lifting. He laughed at my mess and said I was wasting too much time. I had to get back to work. He will have another pile of old wood for me tomorrow. I have come home to shower until long after there was no more hot water but I will never feel clean. I will drink Pilsner until I forget."

"Only in sleep will you forget or feel clean," I said. "Let me put you to bed."

"There is nothing for me in bed. I have no more dreams."

"Let me put you to bed, Father." I put his arm over my shoulder and helped him into the bedroom, turned out the light and took off his clothes.

Parents and teachers, but especially parents, have the ultimate power; they have the trust of innocent minds. The perversion of this trust lies at the root of some of the world's greatest evil. Even the best parents leave a legacy for their children to work through. For children of the worst parents, this is an impossible task.

At school, Tom was the most violent result of misguided authority. He came into school during the reign of the authoritarian prince. At the age of 10, Tom was no taller than a seven-year-old; his body was tight and dry like that of an old man. In his eyes, there was no innocence. His father, a famous sports figure, had brought him to school on his first day.

"I try to give him the strength of a man," his father had said to the prince. "Don't spoil him."

Tom had repulsed any attempt to get close to him. He would drool and let the snot run from his nose to his chin. His temper could crack with the violence of lightning. A child that had attempted to pull him from the climbing bars had been throttled breathless and had been left with a blue welt around his neck.

"Keep that kid in school and you may be responsible for a corpse one day," one of the mothers had said to the prince.

Tom was sent to me daily for observation. I had him draw and was amazed to see that I could recognise the figures in his drawings. Very quickly, he could pick out the distinguishing features of a person and, with a few lines, make them recognisable on paper. I was also concerned to see that, although recognisable, all of his figures had some exaggerated and horrible element that made them monstrous. The first drawing that he did for me showed him with an enormous spear driving it into the bloody behind of his father. I called in his mother, who had the same tight, dry look as her son. She told me that he didn't put on weight because he had terrible problems with constipation and compensated by eating very little. She had been to endless specialists but had found nothing that would really help. Since she had the same problem, most specialists concluded that there was some genetic problem with digestion. His IQ was very high in tests that I gave him. But his emotions were one dimensional; rage, particularly against authority, dominated his thoughts. A personal confrontation between Tom and the prince had ended with the prince throwing him into a chair in order to get his attention and keep him in his office. We were worried that he came to school armed after that so we called in his parents and asked them to keep him at home for three days so that he could cool off. After he came back to school, I made sure to be in the entry every morning to greet him when he came in. After a week, he seemed normal enough, so I allowed myself other distractions in the morning. Not long after, he stabbed the art teacher with a pair of scissors when she made him change what he was drawing. We arranged for him to go to a special programme for difficult and delinquent children after that. We thought that we were finished with him.

A few months later, at the end of a day, the prince collapsed on my couch. "Tom was back in school! Tried to kill me, the little bastard!"

I stood up, walked around my desk to sit next to the prince on the couch. "Are you okay? Is everyone okay? What happened?"

"I am not okay," he said, "but I am not hurt. Nobody is hurt! He was around the kids at the playing field. I had to go down to see what he was doing. But when I got close, he stuck a gun up my ass and asked me if it gave me the strength of a man. He took this small gun from the pocket of his trench coat, from a trench coat, like he was some avenger or something! Asked me if it gave me the strength of a man!"

"What did you do? Is everyone okay?" I asked again. He stood up and then sat down again, his hands rubbing together and then rubbing his knees. "We need to get you to a doctor."

I said, "How did you stop him?"

"Linda saved me. But she didn't even know there was a problem. I was scared. Tom pushed the barrel, painfully, further in. I could already see myself splattered on the fence in front of me.

"I was bent over the fence and saw the arrival of little Linda, coming from the front to give me her hug, her face just above the level of fire. She was on the other side of the short wood fence and could not see the gun." The prince took a few deep breaths and leant back in the couch. "She thought Tom was giving me a hug. She told him that hugging me always made her feel better, that she liked to give me all the hugs she could never give her father. Tom was distracted a bit and surprised by Linda butting in. He asked her where her father was. Linda told him that he was killed in a war. I could feel the pressure of the pistol decrease and was just waiting for the right moment to grab it.

"Tom snapped that he wished his dad was dead. He shoved the gun into me again and said that all he wanted to do was to kill his father. Linda reached over the fence and put a hand softly at the base of Tom's neck. She told him that he couldn't hate the prince. With her hand at the base of his neck, I felt his hands hesitate. She put both her arms around his neck, over the fence. His hands slowly fell and I turned and quickly took away the gun, snapped his arm sharply behind his back and brought the bastard to the office and called the police—and his parents." The prince leant forward with his elbows on his knees, stood up, tottered and nearly fell back down.

"Fucking kid better stay in prison for the rest of his life!"

I took the prince to the hospital, but of course, there wasn't much that they could do.

He was to leave the school soon after that.

Tom spent eight years in a reform school, developing his vicious talent as an artist. Linda visited him often, very often. Linda was certainly born with a propensity for sweetness, but it had been refined and had allowed her to survive in the harshest of environments. With Tom, she was persistent, over years, with soft pressure, like water flowing over granite. Tom was born with only sharp edges, but somehow, she was able to bring out his best, smoothing the cutting crystals and helping them shine.

Chapter 9
Vision Quest

In 1974, I finished my studies in psychology. I was living alone. Petr had gone on to Canada. My father called to congratulate me. He said he had raised his glass in my honour several times already and would like to take me out to dinner, but I declined. He had encouraged me to leave. "Why don't you follow Petr to Canada?" he had asked one night before he had taken his first drink. He was still a target for the government. Both of us knew that if I left, they would probably put him in prison. Maybe it was a sacrifice he was willing to make.

In the end, I packed a picnic for the day. I took my mother's jewellery and some of our glassware to sell along the way. I took the train to a border town and walked through the woods into Germany. The German fields were well kept and the roads nearly new. I felt lighter than I had in years. With a few months' work in Germany, I paid for my flight to Vancouver.

Petr picked me up at the Vancouver Airport. After a long hug, he lowered his head and said, "You will hear people refer to me by my English name. Please call me Peter in the future."

"Ah, Petr, in any case, denial comes naturally to that name," I replied with little energy. I heard myself mumble, "Denial comes naturally to that name," twice more softly.

I was exhausted after 16 hours of flights and transfers. It was raining in Vancouver. We slipped quickly through the city and then drove through forests shrouded in mist as the rain pounded on the windshield and the windshield washers slapped back and forth like parallel metronomes. Peter was talking about his work at a clinic that specialised in rehabilitating celebrity alcoholics. They were using LSD to lead the patients to a personal awareness of their unhealthy lifestyles.

As we made our way through mossy forests of ancient trees, Peter told me about the famous people he had met and the enlightenment that he had gone through with LSD. I had the impression that I was passing from one form of 'normalisation' to another.

We stopped in front of a massive log house in the midst of dense woods. I had never seen cedars so tall, straight and thick. They formed a green wall around the building that reminded me of the fortifications around medieval cities in Europe.

In front of the building was an enormous totem of strangely carved images stacked on top of one another. On the bottom was an enormous bear supporting the weight of the entire column. On the top was an eagle about to take flight.

The interior of the hospital was all wood. Large windows and cathedral ceilings in the entrance gave the feeling of entering a temple except that the light was all green against the brown grain of wood. All of the glass windows were stained by the colour of the surrounding forest.

"I have arranged a room for you," Peter said with hesitation, perhaps waiting for a response. "One of your own, just next to mine. Would you like a drink at the bar before I show you up?"

My fatigue and the change of reality from Czechoslovakia to Germany and then to Canada had me feeling spread through time and space. I hadn't psychologically left Czechoslovakia. Yet, I felt still adrift above the earth somewhere, waiting for a landing.

"I think that I could sleep for a year. Please take me up to the bedroom," I replied.

I had a little room in what must have once been an attic, now converted into a small, rectangular bedroom with a single bed, a dresser, a sink with a mirror above and, at the end of the room, a beautiful dormer window looking out into the trees.

I put down my bags, took off my coat and shoes and lay down directly on the bed. I remember falling asleep to the exquisite feeling of having my aching feet rubbed by Peter as he talked about the clinic.

When I awoke, it was dark. I had no idea where I was or what time of night it could be. I stood up but lost my balance, caught hold of the sink, felt for the faucets and ran cold water over my hands and splashed my face. I heard rain falling and felt my way in the dark towards the window and opened it up. The in-rushing air was filled with the smell of wet wood. The rain had a sound like no other rain that I had ever heard. It was hushed, damped, silenced by branch after mossy branch as it fell finally, if it made it to the ground at all, on prehistoric fern and moss. I was nowhere, I recognised—no sound of hard rain on cobbled European streets, no city noises to overpower the rain. I was in a fortress of forest with walls older than those in medieval cities.

The organic smell of growth and rot was witness to the rampant pace of wild life.

I left the window open and stumbled back to my bed and lay for hours as shadows slowly formed and a new day dawned in muffled forest light.

A knock on the door was followed by the leaping entrance of Peter. He dropped a small backpack on the floor, hopped onto the bed and said, "Wake up, lazy bones. I have packed a picnic so we could take a walk in the woods."

We walked along a path worn into thick moss through woods of cedar trees that made me feel like a small child, tiny in proportion to the surrounding spaces. The light was every shade of green with occasional star-spangled spaces of white flowers. Ferns rose to the heights of our heads and slugs the size of small cucumbers oozed their way across the trail. "It must be easy to get lost in these woods," I said to Peter. "Are there wild animals in this wilderness?"

"The trails are easy to follow. I know my way around," Peter replied. "There are bears, and every once in a while, someone sites a mountain lion. But if we make noise as we go, both would rather avoid us than bother us. Neither of them would be as dangerous as the Soviet bear and its destruction of all Czechs."

We walked for several hours. Peter led the way without hesitation past many splits in the trail.

The only landmarks that I could make out were fallen trees, stumps, roots and hillsides that all seemed the same. I felt a bit like a sailor without a sextant surrounded by the immense, undifferentiated landscape of a green sea.

We did at last come to a huge clearing, a clear cut in the woods that must have been made by loggers several years before. The huge stumps of trees showing, like footprints, the tracks of the enormous trees that had been there before. We climbed on the top of one of the flattened stumps, big enough to lie down on without touching either end. The sun on the blackened stump made it warm. It seemed to steam in its humidity with the heat.

Peter opened his pack and took out a long sausage, a loaf of bread and a bottle of water. We cut slices of bread and sausage and ate them on our wooden slab. I was tired from the walk and jetlag. I took off my sweater, my shoes and socks and lay back to sleep with my sweater under my head. Peter lay perpendicular to me and put his head on my stomach as a pillow. It was warm in the sun. I was exhausted. I fell into sleep like a hot spoon slips into honey.

I dreamt of an explorer slashing his way through tropical jungle. I saw the sweating—dirty back of a man in front of me as he cut us a path through trackless jungle. Vines and branches pulled at us from every side and soggy soil sucked the shoes right off our feet. I felt ensnared, entangled in endless undergrowth. I leant forward and put my hands on the sweating back of the man in front of me. The head turned, and I saw the face of my father.

My eyes opened to see Peter on his side next to me, with his hands sliding beneath my shirt and pants. "I was dreaming of my father," I said. "We were lost in the jungle and caught by grabbing vines."

"We are not lost. Put your thoughts and bad dreams away. Relax in the silence of this wilderness and forget your father." I could not relax in the touch but enjoyed a silence more powerful than any I had ever heard. I closed my eyes but felt only dark images. The loud snap of a breaking branch stained the silence. I opened my eyes and screamed as I saw the head of a bear come over the edge of the tree trunk. It swung a huge brown paw at Peter's back and knocked him off the trunk into the bushes. I rolled off the trunk backwards, landing with my head down in a blackberry bush and scrambled through the thorns in panic. Peter jumped to his feet, and we ran through the bushes. We heard nothing behind us and glanced back to see the bear on the stump finishing the last bits of our sausage. We ran again, thinking that it would come after us when no food was left. We found a path and ran until we could no longer breathe. Bent over double, gasping for breath, I could see Peter's torn and bloody back in front of me. His jean jacket was ripped from the centre of the back to the side of his waist, and blood oozed through the fabric.

"Let me look at your back," I said. I pulled aside the tattered cloth and found four shallow grooves like bloody furrows in a freshly ploughed field. But the bleeding wasn't bad.

"How does it look?" Peter asked.

"You were lucky; it is not too deep, but we do need to find a doctor to stitch you up," I said.

So we ran and walked, walked and ran. I followed Peter with no idea of where I was going, but as we continued, I had less and less impression that he knew where we were as well.

He stopped and fell to his knees. Shock was setting in, and he began sobbing and shaking. I put my hand on his head and started to shout and call but the sounds seemed to disappear into the muffled softness of the growth around us.

"It is no use screaming for help in Czech," Peter said.
"What should we do?" I asked.

Peter rolled himself into a ball and rocked back and forth on his feet. After a long moment, he said, "My back is on fire."

Then I heard a soft voice behind me. We turned to see a short native woman with soft brown eyes, her ears pierced with a row of rings in natural stone, dark hair over her shoulder.

"You must be from the clinic, too many trips on LSD and not enough walks in the woods. I better take you back and tell them to keep you inside where you'll stay out of trouble." She spoke slowly as if she was speaking to children, so even with my little English, I was able to understand. We followed, relieved to have her help.

We were led quickly back to the clinic, where one of the doctors stitched Peter up. "You'll be sleeping on your stomach for a while," he said, "but count yourself lucky."

We quietly ate some dinner and then Peter walked me up to my room. "Tomorrow we will go on another trip," he said. "Or you will go and I will be your guide. The woods that I will take you into will be wilder than we saw today, but this time, I won't let you get lost. In the land of LSD, I am a trustworthy guide."

"Please don't let me get lost again, Peter. I don't know if I will find a sweet-eyed native to bring me home. I want to go to the place that brings my mind to the peace that I saw in her muddy brown eyes. I felt like I was staring into the infinite swirls of the Vlatva River. I am not sure a pill can take me to such a place. She looked like she found her peace outside," I said. "My mother is the only other person that I have seen with eyes like that." I looked at Peter but his eyes shifted to the floor.

"On LSD, you can crawl inside your mother's eyes and find the foundations of her peace," he said. He was seated, hands rubbing his thighs and his knee shook in place.

In the morning, Peter took me to the trip room, gave me a drink, massaged my neck and spoke words I have since forgotten, softly to me. Mozart's horn concertos were on the stereo. I settled into a corner stuffed with soft red pillows. The room had the look of a brothel but I closed my eyes and concentrated on the music. It felt like a welcoming to heaven, my body resonated, at one with the ringing horns. I felt myself vibrating in tune to God's tones. I was one with the universe, non-localised in time and space, ecstatic for a very long time.

But then there was change. There was a slowing of time that made movement seem thick and viscous like the flow of old oil. I saw myself walking through dense forest with my father, displaced from a geography of Czechoslovakia to one of British Columbia with rainforest undergrowth thick with fern and berries. We walked hand-in-hand, looking at the ground, searching for something. Under a thicket of fern, we found an emerging white mushroom, its thick head on a narrow stalk arising from the mossy bed of the ground. My father held it in his hand and had me open my mouth as he fed it to me. There were many of them, and my father took them one by one and fed them slowly to me. One of them opened and, as I took it into my mouth, it seemed to release its spoors. I felt the taste of musty rot. I felt the tendril arms of the underground mycelium, feeding on dead material. I saw the crawling worms and the degradation and felt myself turning to earth. I screamed and screamed and refused a hand that I thought was forcing me to eat more. Never has time seemed so long. I did finally open my eyes to a room that still looked like a brothel but with a gaze that saw it as the red fires of hell. I was on my knees with my head in Peter's lap as he stroked my hair and told me he could keep me from harm.

"I brought you home safely this time," Peter said.

"The safety of hell," I replied. "I saw the twisted connections between life and death. Growth and decay inseparable, my father's touch turn to rot. I saw no sign of my mother's eyes. My life is only feed for worms… Life is only feed for worms."

"Again your father robs you of a chance for peace," Peter said. "Again the hero is a monster. What is the story behind this? In what abuse did he plant his seed to have it turn to rot? You have only one way home. Point your pistol at your father and pull the trigger. You must walk over his dead body to find the peace and life in your mother's eyes."

"My father was my foundation; he held me up. He was the solid ground. My mother is spirit, air, peace. My father is… my father is…"

I was locked in a dark room, seeing only vague shapes. I shook an old brass door handle reflecting dull gold light in the dim room. The handle came off in my hands and the door was impossible to open. I stumbled and groped through the corners of a room with the smell and the feel of a root cellar—must, decay, cold stones and humidity. I was cold and curled up in a corner and rocked myself to the most unrestful, endlessly agitated sleep with a repeating dream.

I see the powerful rear flanks of a buck as it drove its sex into a doe. I would see the big doe eyes wide in fright and excitement. The forelimbs of the male animal were the claws of a bear, and it would rake the flanks of the doe as they coupled. The doe would try to pull away but, evidently, the knot of the male was too swollen, making the couple inseparable. I would watch the thrusting male and the impaled female for what seemed like a very long time. They would separate and I would see the huge drooping penis, still pulsating and dripping a yellowish, red fluid. I would awake with a scream as my eyes would turn to the head of the male beast. In the dream, I feel that I know the human face, but visually, it is not clear—a smeared vision as if through mottled, misty glass.

I spent several weeks in delirium in a hospital after my trip on LSD. Apparently, Peter had spent much of the first week with me. But a beautiful, rich client came for treatment at the clinic at that time, and Peter disappeared quickly from my life.

I left the hospital and went to the orchards in central British Columbia to pick fruit. I spent the summer and fall outside in the orchards and in the woods. By winter, my mind felt almost clear and, with luck, I found my job as a school psychologist soon after. Work has since been my salvation. I have listened to stories and have slowly buried my own.

I learnt later that they did put my father in prison. The news that I could get told me that he stayed in prison for a year. Two years after my arrival in Canada, I received a letter from the Czech government telling me that he was dead. They had taken all of his belongings but they wrote that if I wanted them, I could come claim them.

For 25 years now, I have been a dream-catcher, listening to the problems of others. I can get close to children, and I work with their parents to limit the damage that life can cause.

Hundreds of children have grown and graduated with my guidance. The best of the stories have shown that frustration and aggression can make important tools for creativity.

Linda, as an adult, is often in the news for running a farm where the homeless, mostly young drug addicts and prostitutes, can come to work. In the fresh air with responsibility for animals and plants, many of them find some ground to walk on. Tom comes to help her on occasion but mostly, we read about him as an artist. His paintings of twisted figures in various levels of bondage have become very famous. I have a copy of one that I keep to myself but I am told that it's worth more than the cost of my car.

Not long ago, I visited Linda on the farm. We picked apples and she started to ask me about my past. "It must have been difficult growing up in Communist Czechoslovakia," she said.

"Czechs have lived 40 years of someone else's history," I replied. "Most of us do not want to look back, and I seem unable to."

"It is dangerous driving with no rearview mirror," she replied. "You know better than I that repressed memories build up like the blast from an ultrasonic airplane. They come after we see the jet but they can shatter the windows and shake the walls."

"It is better to be hit by a sonic boom than by the plane that creates it," I replied with little conviction.

"There is a sick old man, that speaks mostly Czech, living down on the streets. He probably needs to be in a hospital but he refuses to go. I would like to try to get him on to the farm.

"Perhaps you could help me and perhaps he has some stories that could help you," Linda said. I had no interest in meeting an old Czech man but I couldn't refuse to help Linda. So, we made a meeting time to go downtown and try to find the homeless Czech. We would meet at Tom's studio and then go out on the street."

Chapter 10
Oppression and Creativity

"In a world of global civilisation, only those who are looking for a technical trick to save that civilisation need despair. But those who believe, in all modesty, in the mysterious power of their own human being, which mediates between them and the mysterious power of the world's being, have no reason to despair at all."
Vaclav Havel

Linda, Tom and I met in the morning at Tom's studio/gallery. He was in the chic section of Vancouver surrounded by law offices and the shopping district. The front of the place was a gallery hung with huge paintings mostly in black, white and red that showed bound and often wrapped women and men in provocative positions of constraint and submission. His painting had improved in technique since he was a child, but the themes were nearly the same. It seemed to be a theme with resonance for many others because I was told that he sold better than any other artist in Vancouver and that he did very well internationally.

We went to the back for coffee in a well-lit studio with easels, stacks of canvases and an enormous computer.

"You are holding your psychosis hostage for profit," I said.

"I share the psychosis with the rest of the world, and we seem to revel in it. The history of humanity is one of power and submission. The world should be happy that I have turned away from rage, and have, with the help of Linda, learnt to speak for the sensitive submissive side," Tom responded in a soft voice with a slight smile.

"The meek shall inherit the Earth, but what state will it be in by the time of the inheritance? Are there more positive responses to power than submission?" Tom's calmness angered me. I felt my blood rise. I saw my father's rage and frustration drowned by alcohol, and I saw Tom's ease with his violent past made possible by pouring the violence onto canvas.

"You tell me, Dream Catcher. We can blow up the world in anger or submit and create with all of that energy," Tom said.

"In Czechoslovakia, I have been witness to true stories of successful passive resistance that wasn't submission," I replied, struggling to support an argument that still seemed unclear.

"I have never heard you talk about them," Linda said.

"Dream Catcher only listens to stories," Tom said. "Maybe someday she will tell us one."

"My stories are like dreams, even to myself. I know that they are important, but I do not know what they mean. I would rather forget most of my stories, but maybe it is time for me to start telling them to those who mean the most to me," I replied. "I am not sure that I can put them together myself yet. I need something to shake the pieces into place."

"Perhaps if you and the old man talk together, you can put those pieces together," Linda said. "Let's take a thermos of coffee and try to lure the old man home. What does he look like?" I asked.

"He is tall with long white hair and a beard, both still showing a tinge of blonde. He walks around the university and down by the port. The police have picked him up once but they couldn't communicate very well because he speaks mostly Czech. He stays out of the way and seems to take care of himself, so they tend to leave him alone, but they did tell me about him and I have met him once. I think I was able to communicate to him that I would like to take him out to the farms but he clearly indicated he didn't want to leave the city."

We spent all of the morning looking with no luck. We ate sandwiches in a café at lunch, and just as we were about to pay, I turned to look up the street behind me and saw a long-haired man staring at me from the other side of the street. I stood up too quickly. My head seemed to spin. All went black. When I opened my eyes, I looked up into a circle of faces—out of focus. One caught my attention with a look beyond recognition. I saw long hair, a beard and the eyes of my father. I closed my eyes again but I felt his hand on my forehead and heard his voice in Czech give me the wakeup call that I had heard every morning of my childhood: "It is morning time, jewel. Wipe the dreams away," he said in Czech.

Chapter 11
Reflections

A human action becomes genuinely important when it springs from the soil of a clear-sighted awareness of the temporality and the ephemerality of everything human."
Vaclav Havel

"How can you still be alive, Father?" I think I asked.

"You kept me alive," he replied.

"But the government wrote me a letter telling me that you were dead."

"The government wanted me dead, and in those days, I wanted to die. It was the best arrangement for all of us. Perhaps they were stupid enough to think that you would come home."

The constructions of my adult world had just lost their foundations. I felt myself crumble and fall. I am told that I passed a second several weeks in delirium. And I dreamt, mixtures of upset and confusion. I remember images of a lungfish, slimy and soft-bellied, emerging from muddy, brackish water, gasping for its first breaths of air. I could only just breathe and had only the speck of a brain, so I slept. And re-emerged in dreams of awaking in a darkened room, I could feel cold stone edges of the corner of the room. The room felt and sounded expansive. There were the echoes and air currents of a massive, cathedral-like space. With the help of these solid stone walls, I stood and turned away from the darkened corner towards a centre that was bright with sunlight filtered from above. I reached a hand towards the light, one hand still bracing me against the wall. My father walked slowly into the lighted centre from the shadows on the opposite side. The wall was cold to the touch of my hand; I moved towards the light, following the outstretched hand, leaving the support of the cold stone. I clasped hands with my father, and we embraced in a circle of light.

When I awoke, I was in a hospital bed in a bare room on my own. I was sure that I was just coming out of another bad trip at the clinic. I was only surprised to see my aged father come into my hospital room. He took my hand, and I resisted, pulling away.

"Do not be afraid of me. I am not a ghost," he said.

"I have been living with your ghost for years," I replied.

"You pulled away from me before you left," he said.

"I couldn't talk to you. You were an abusive alcoholic."

"I was an alcoholic, so I certainly abused myself. That hurt everyone and everything around me."

"Do you have any idea what pushed me away?"

"You are the psychologist, I believe. You tell me."

"I couldn't stand your touch because it was untrustworthy."

"I was completely out of touch once your mother died," he replied. "Do you not remember an inappropriate touch? I know that I was drunk most evenings after your mother died but no amount of drink would drive me to abuse you."

"Alcohol and age have taken your memory. The memory of you turned my own therapy to hell at the clinic."

"Are you sure that the memory did not come from the therapy? The clinic, it sounds like another factory for well-planned, emotional images."

"The clinic just unearthed my repressed memory. Work has allowed me to go beyond it."

"It doesn't sound like you have gone much beyond it. I haven't been to a hospital for therapy, unless prison qualifies. Alcoholism was harder to escape and is more devastating than prison, but my incarceration allowed me eventually to dry out enough to feel free. The strength that I needed to leave both bonds behind came from a desire to see you again before I died. Of all that I believed in as a young man, the only feeling that remains is the certainty that I care for you and your mother."

If we wake during dreaming, the dream stays with us. If we wake outside of dreamtime, the dream is lost. Dreams and memories are creations, both built on the shifting sands of the mind and time. I sometimes speculate about the possibility of reincarnation and wonder if the passage between lives is like the period between dreams. We wake in a new life, having completely forgotten about the previous one. One can feel multiple memories, fractured like light coming through a kaleidoscope, and we remould and remodel them, trying to piece together the initial beam. On occasions, I have had flashes that felt like transcendence of memory into pure experience. At those times, my soul rings with mercy and forgiveness.

"You can no longer carry me on your shoulders, Papa, and I can no longer carry you in my memories. What do we have to hold us up?"

"Take my hand and let us tell each other stories," he said.

Ingram Content Group UK Ltd.
Milton Keynes UK
UKHW020631230423
420621UK00013B/1678